WATCH
ME
OUTDOORS

Grateful acknowledgement is made to the Los Angeles City School District, the Lassen Elementary School, their kindergarten classes and teachers for permission to photograph.

Red wooden car by Creative Playthings

First Printing . . . . .June 1967
Second Printing . . . . .November 1968

Bowmar Early Childhood Series

WATCH ME OUTDOORS

written by Ruth Jaynes

photographed by Harvey Mandlin

Bowmar Publishing Corp.
Glendale, California

"Watch me!" says Denny.

"I'm pouring water into the dry sand.

"The water makes the sand wet.
I'm patting it with my hand.

"I'm making something in the wet sand.
I'm building it up high. It's a high mountain.
Higher, higher, higher.

"My red car goes up the mountain.
Up, up, up.

"My red car goes down the mountain.

Down, down, down.

"Watch me!" says Denny.

"I'm digging a tunnel through the mountain.

Dig, dig, dig.

"My red car goes into the tunnel. It's gone. Where's my red car?

"Here it comes, out the other side.

"Watch me!" says Denny.

"I'm making a big, wide road. It's a highway.

"My red car goes on the highway.
Zoom! Zoom! Zoom!

"Watch me!" says Denny.

"It's time to put my red car away. I back it up slowly.
Back, back, back, out of the sand.

"Now it's parked safely inside on the shelf.

Good-bye, red car. I'll see you tomorrow."

The End

PICTURE BOOKS IN THE BOWMAR EARLY CHILDHOOD SERIES

Part One:
ABOUT MYSELF

Do You Know What...?
Melissa Lou has begun to discover that she is a person of capability and worth, special and distinct from all others as she enjoys her own particular place with the members of her family, her teacher and classmates.

What Is A Birthday Child?
This book shows a little girl experiencing the most important event in a young child's life—her own day—her birthday. Through simple recognition of this day, Juanita, and other children, are helped to see themselves as unique persons, worthy of recognition and celebration.

Father Is Big
The father role is portrayed here in terms that are understandable to the child, through showing *bigness* and strength in exquisite photographs. Even for children from fatherless homes the book pictures an understandable family relationship, and holds hope for the child that he may one day become *big* and achieve his role as a strong family member.

The Littlest House
Living in a very small house, even a tiny mobile home, can be the source of many delightful experiences and lively conversations, as seen in this happy, personal *tour* of "The Littlest House."

The Biggest House
Houses differ, but they all shelter families, and this one shelters many! As one family, among many, living in "the biggest house on the street" Robert tells about all the things he can do, people he can know, and, most of all, about the pride he has in this special place—his home.

Friends! Friends! Friends!
Through the person-to-person relationships depicted in this book, the young child, like Kimi, becomes more aware of friendship experiences in his own classroom.

My Friend is Mrs. Jones
With his adult friend and neighbor a little boy enjoys helping, being helped, and doing things with this sensitive, older companion. Through this relationship children are helped to identify with this child, in verbalizing and in finding ways of their own to be friends.

Part Two:
THE WORLD AROUND ME

Let Me See You Try
Readiness to attempt new tasks of physical involvement are encouraged through the joyful participation of many children as they skip, clap, tiptoe and as they ask questions, such as, "Can you skip in a circle?" and add, "Let me see you try!"

My Tricycle and I
A tricycle ride with the little boy in the story encourages children to develop a greater awareness of many basic physical and sensory learnings. At the same time the imaginative delights of a *pretend* ride, at the child's level of pretence, is explored.

Watch Me Outdoors
Children in the sand box, sharing Denny's experiences, will become more aware of the sensory and imaginative uses of sand and water. They will be involved in the best of learning situations for the young child, *play*.

Watch Me Indoors
The enthusiasm of a little girl showing her special visitor—her mother—all the things she can do at school will help children everywhere to identify with and enjoy more their expanding store of accomplishments.

Follow The Leader
As the children in this story enthusiastically participate in important motor development, they gradually learn how to use and control their bodies, at the same time reinforcing the language development that so often accompanies this type of learning through play.

Melinda's Christmas Stocking
Melinda's immediate world takes on new meaning as she sees, touches, smells, hears and tastes the various objects she finds in her Christmas stocking.

Listen!
An introduction to some of the sounds commonly heard in the places children commonly go — the park, the city, school and home. Greater interest in and sensitivity to these and other sounds in our environment is encouraged through the delightful presentation in this basic book of sounds.

A Box Tied with a Red Ribbon
All the children try to guess what is in the box that Nancy brings to school. "Is it a toy?" "Can we play with it?" They shake the box. They open it. The surprise box excites all five senses as the children explore all the possibilities of its contents.

An Apple is Red
How does an apple look when you bite it? When you dry a grape, does it still look like a grape? Keener observation of shape, color and taste are invited and encouraged through the esthetic presentation of beginning science concepts.

Part Three:
I TALK—I THINK—I REASON

What Do You Say?
Many ways of saying the same thing are introduced through the visit of two children and a friendly adult to a supermarket carnival. The child hears his own vocabulary used and at the same time is introduced to new expressions equally usable.

Furry Boy
As the children take care of a pet rabbit this stimulating environment brings about much real language development. Their love and growing reliability as they care for Furry Boy is also apparent in every word and picture.

Tell Me, Please! What's That?
David speaks English. Juan speaks Spanish. The different kinds of animals in the Children's Zoo motivate David and Juan to talk, and the vocabulary of each is expanded as the boys understand and use the other's language.

Funny Mr. Clown
While increasing their capacity for humor through real experiences and the preposterous statement, the children are finding joy in seeing a clown do tricks for their own class.

Benny's Four Hats
Observations and comparisons by children are always necessary in the building of ideas and growth in ability to reason. As Benny puts on, and wears each of his hats, children will use these meaningful tools in *guessing* why Benny wears each hat, and then *seeing* why he did in the story.

Where Is Whiffen?
Both reasoning and persistence are demonstrated at a child's level of understanding as Jimmy tries to find his dog, Whiffen. After several unsuccessful attempts to find Whiffen, Jimmy arrives at a successful solution.

That's What It Is!
A lively curiosity is the basis for the desire to learn, and in this book, Marcus' actions show that his curiosity has been encouraged. Children, as they enjoy Marcus' adventure will become more curious, themselves, will want to explore, to investigate, to question.

Do You Suppose Miss Riley Knows?
On his most important day, his birthday, Rudy wonders if his teacher will remember. Gradually, through all the special occurrences, he reasons that she *must* know and finally that she *does* know.

A Beautiful Day For a Picnic
A beautiful day, a packed lunch, a long, long walk, play in the sunshine, eating lunch outdoors—these are a picnic! The formation of a concept begins to occur, when with adult help children begin to relate information around a core idea.

Colors
Although children grow up in a world surrounded by color, too many live from day to day totally unaware of its beauty, variety and excitement. The book, "Colors", presents all three of these elements—beauty, variety and excitement—in such a way as to inspire maximum carryover into the live world of color around us.

Three Baby Chicks
Three children show their fascination with the ending of a long classroom vigil—the hatching of three baby chicks! To the very young child whose world must often seem to be made of magic the unfolding of events such as this begin to help him reason, to interpret and to understand how and why things happen.

I Like Cats
The concepts that begin to form in a child's mind about the variety of behavior of similar animals is strengthened as the little girl in this story shows her obvious pleasure in cats, and particularly in *her* cat.

Morning
What does *morning* mean to a child? Out of the thousands of early-in-the-day experiences every child has, some have come to mean morning. This story sorts out some of these commonly shared experiences and helps children to a greater awareness of morning.

Evening
What makes *evening*? The routine things that families do at this time of the day are delightfully pictured in this book where every page expresses the love and security that all children need.

Bowmar Publishing Corp.
Glendale, California

JUNIOR BIOS

Chris Hemsworth

BY HAYLEY NORRIS

Enslow
PUBLISHING

Please visit our website, www.enslow.com. For a free color catalog of all our high-quality books, call toll free 1-800-398-2504 or fax 1-877-980-4454.

Cataloging-in-Publication Data

Names: Norris, Hayley.
Title: Chris Hemsworth / Hayley Norris.
Description: New York : Enslow Publishing, 2021. | Series: Junior bios | Includes glossary and index.
Identifiers: ISBN 9781978518810 (pbk.) | ISBN 9781978518834 (library bound) | ISBN 9781978518827 (6 pack)
Subjects: LCSH: Hemsworth, Chris–Juvenile literature. | Actors–Australia–Biography–Juvenile literature.
Classification: LCC PN3018.H457 N667 2021 | DDC 792.0'28'092 B–dc23

Published in 2021 by
Enslow Publishing
101 West 23rd Street, Suite #240
New York, NY 10011

Designer: Sarah Liddell
Editor: Kate Mikoley

Photo credits: Cover, p. 1 (Chris Hemsworth) lev radin/Shutterstock.com; cover, p. 1 (photo frame) Aleksandr Andrushkiv/Shutterstock.com; marble texture used throughout HardtIllustrations/Shutterstock.com; lined paper texture used throughout Mtsaride/Shutterstock.com; watercolor texture used throughout solarbird/Shutterstock.com; p. 5 Barry King/Contributor/Getty Images Entertainment/Getty Images; p. 7 C. Uncle/Staff/FilmMagic/Getty Images; p. 9 Kevin Winter/Staff/Getty Images Entertainment/Getty Images; p. 11 Mark Metcalfe/Getty Images Entertainment/Getty Images; p. 12 Albert L. Ortega/Getty Images Entertainment/Getty Images; p. 15 ANGELA WEISS/Contributor/AFP/Getty Images; p. 17 Steve Granitz/Contributor/WireImage/Getty Images; p. 19 Brook Mitchell/Stringer/Getty Images Entertainment/Getty Images.

Portions of this work were originally authored by Alex Malley and published as *Chris Hemsworth*. All new material this edition authored by Hayley Norris.

Printed in the United States of America

Some of the images in this book illustrate individuals who are models. The depictions do not imply actual situations or events.

CPSIA compliance information: Batch #BS20ENS: For further information contact Enslow Publishing, New York, New York, at 1-800-542-2595.

Find us on 📘 📷

Contents

Australia to Avenger 4

Getting into Acting 6

Becoming Thor 10

Making More Movies 14

Family Man 16

Giving to Others 18

Soap Opera to Superhero 20

Chris's Timeline 21

Glossary 22

For More Information 23

Index 24

Words in the glossary appear in **bold** type
the first time they are used in the text.

Australia to Avenger

Today, Chris Hemsworth is one of the most famous actors in the movie business. You might know him as the superhero Thor from the many *Avengers* movies he's been in. However, Chris's journey to fame started long before he was Thor.

Chris was born in Melbourne, Australia, on August 11, 1983. His mother, Leonie, was a teacher. His father, Craig, worked in social services. Chris has two brothers, Luke and Liam. They're both actors too! Chris is the middle child in his family. Luke is older and Liam is younger. When Chris was young, the family moved around Australia a few times.

4

Liam

Chris

Luke

CHRIS HAS SAID THAT PLAYING PRETEND WITH HIS BROTHERS AS A KID HELPED HIM BECOME THE ACTOR HE IS TODAY.

5

Getting into Acting

Chris was interested in movies and TV from a young age. He became interested in acting when he was in high school. His brother Luke was acting in an Australian **soap opera**, and Chris started to see that he, too, could work as an actor.

FACTS BEHIND THE FIGURE

Chris has said that part of the reason he started acting was that he wanted to help his family with money. He even helped his parents pay off their house.

CHRIS WORKED ON *HOME AND AWAY* UNTIL 2007, WHEN HE DECIDED TO TRY ACTING IN THE UNITED STATES.

Chris had a few small **roles** on TV shows in 2002 and 2003, but his big break came in 2004. Following in his older brother's footsteps, Chris got a job playing one of the regular characters on an Australian soap opera. He moved to Sydney, Australia, to film the show, called *Home and Away*.

7

Once he moved to the United States, Chris began trying out for movie roles in the center of the film business—Hollywood, California. He landed a small part in the 2009 movie, *Star Trek*.

Still, Chris was having a hard time getting acting jobs. He was going to lots of **auditions**, but not getting any big parts. He would get nervous before auditions and has said he thought about quitting and moving back to Australia.

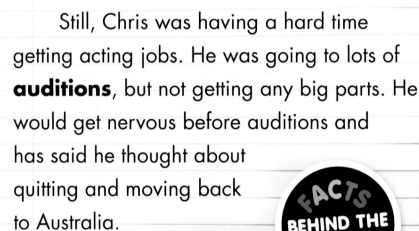

FACTS BEHIND THE FIGURE

In myths, Thor is known as a powerful god. In Marvel movies, Thor is a superhero known as the God of Thunder. He has a large hammer he uses to destroy things. Chris had to become very fit to play the role.

CHRIS'S YOUNGER BROTHER LIAM
ALSO TRIED OUT TO PLAY THOR!

Instead, he kept on auditioning. His hard work paid off. He landed the role of the title character in the 2011 Marvel movie, *Thor*.

Becoming Thor

Playing Thor was a turning point in Chris's career. He was **nominated** for a few awards, or honors, for his role in the 2011 movie, but that wasn't the end of Thor for Chris. He's continued playing the role in several other Marvel movies.

FACTS BEHIND THE FIGURE

People loved Chris as Thor. He went on to play the character in more Marvel movies, including *Thor: The Dark World* (2013), *Avengers: Age of Ultron* (2015), and *Thor: Ragnarok* (2017).

THE AVENGERS ARE A GROUP OF SUPERHEROES, INCLUDING THOR, IRON MAN, CAPTAIN AMERICA, AND THE HULK. CHRIS IS SHOWN HERE WITH MARK RUFFALO, WHO PLAYS THE HULK.

In 2012, Chris brought back his role as Thor in the popular movie, *The Avengers*. This was the highest-**grossing** movie of the year. This movie brought more nominations for Chris—and two wins. He won a Teen Choice Award for the favorite male summer movie star. He also shared an MTV Movie Award for Best Fight with some of his **costars**.

BEFORE PLAYING THOR, CHRIS HAD TRIED OUT FOR A FEW OTHER ROLES THAT HE DIDN'T GET. IF HE HADN'T KEPT TRYING, HE NEVER WOULD HAVE BECOME THOR!

Thor: Ragnarok showed off more of Thor's silly side than the earlier movies had. This gave Chris a chance to use his **comedy** skills.

12

In 2018, Chris played Thor in another *Avengers* movie, *Avengers: Infinity War*. In it, Thor and the other Avengers come together to try to save the world from a **supervillain** named Thanos. When it came out, *Avengers: Infinity War* made more money than any other Marvel movie before it.

The following year, Chris was back playing Thor in *Avengers: Endgame*. This movie made even more money than *Avengers: Infinity War*. After it came out in 2019, it became the highest-grossing movie ever!

In His Own Words
"As a kid, you run around the house pretending to be a superhero, and now to be doing it as a job. I feel very lucky."

Making More Movies

Chris has played Thor in so many movies that it may be hard to imagine him finding time for other roles. But he's done it! Between all the Marvel films Chris has been in, he's also had parts in many other movies.

FACTS BEHIND THE FIGURE

In 2019, Chris starred as the **alien**-fighting Agent H in *Men in Black: International*. The film is a follow-up to a popular **franchise** that started with *Men in Black* in 1997.

IN *MEN IN BLACK: INTERNATIONAL*, CHRIS STARRED ALONGSIDE TESSA THOMPSON, WHO WAS ALSO IN *THOR: RAGNAROK*.

In 2012, Chris played the Huntsman in the movie *Snow White and the Huntsman*. In 2016, he played the character again in the movie, *The Huntsman: Winter's War*. In 2013, Chris played a 1970s race car driver in the movie *Rush*. He's also had roles in other movies, such as *Vacation* and *Ghostbusters*, where he was able to work more on his comedy skills.

Family Man

When he's not acting, Chris likes to surf and play other sports. These activities help him stay in shape to play a superhero!

Chris also enjoys spending time with his family. Chris and his wife Elsa Pataky, who was born in Madrid, Spain, got married in 2010. In 2012, Chris and Elsa had a daughter named India Rose. Two years later, they had twin boys, named Tristan and Sasha.

FACTS BEHIND THE FIGURE

Chris and his family moved back to his home country of Australia around 2014. In 2016, he started working with Tourism Australia, a group that aims to get people from all over the world to visit the country.

CHRIS AND ELSA MET THROUGH THEIR TALENT AGENT. THIS IS A PERSON WHO HELPS ACTORS GET JOBS.

Elsa is an actor too. Like Chris, she's no stranger to movie franchises. Elsa played a character named Elena in several movies in the *Fast & Furious* franchise.

17

Giving to Others

Helping others is important to Chris. He has **donated** money to causes he cares about and uses his fame to help spread the word about charities. One group he works closely with is the Australian Childhood Foundation. This organization works to help children who have been abused, or treated in harmful ways. Chris helps the group raise money and gain support.

In His Own Words

"For me life is about experience and being a good person."

IN 2018, CHRIS HELPED DESIGN A WATCH WITH A COMPANY CALLED TAG HEUER. MONEY FROM THE SALE OF THE WATCH SUPPORTED THE AUSTRALIAN CHILDHOOD FOUNDATION.

A series of harmful bushfires, or uncontrolled fires in bush areas, burned through Australia in 2019 and 2020. Chris announced on social media that he and his family would donate $1 million to help fight these fires. He also encouraged others to donate.

Soap Opera to Superhero

Chris's acting career has come a long way since he started out working on Australian soap operas. And it doesn't look like he'll be handing over the hammer any time soon. In 2019, it was announced that a fourth *Thor* movie, starring Chris, was set to come out in 2021 and would be called *Thor: Love and Thunder*.

Known for playing an on-screen superhero, Chris sometimes likes to step away from the spotlight to spend time with his family. He also uses his fame to help others—that makes him a superhero in more ways than one!

Chris's Timeline

1983: CHRIS IS BORN ON AUGUST 11.

2004: CHRIS STARTS ACTING IN HOME AND AWAY.

2009: CHRIS HAS A PART IN STAR TREK.

2010: CHRIS MARRIES ELSA PATAKY.

2011: THOR COMES OUT.

2012: THE AVENGERS COMES OUT.
CHRIS'S DAUGHTER INDIA IS BORN.

2013: CHRIS PLAYS A 1970S RACE CAR DRIVER IN THE MOVIE RUSH.

2014: CHRIS'S SONS TRISTAN AND SASHA ARE BORN.

2019: AVENGERS: ENDGAME COMES OUT.
MEN IN BLACK: INTERNATIONAL COMES OUT.

2020: CHRIS DONATES $1 MILLION TO HELP FIGHT AUSTRALIAN BUSHFIRES.

Glossary

alien A being from another planet.

audition A try out. Also, to try out for a role.

comedy Things done and said to make viewers laugh.

costar One of two or more main actors in the same movie.

donate To give something to others who need it.

franchise A series of related movies set in the same pretend universe, often with the same characters.

gross To earn an amount of money before expenses are taken into account.

nominate To suggest someone for an honor or award.

role The part a person plays.

soap opera A dramatic TV show that tells ongoing stories about the characters' lives and problems.

supervillain A fictional, or pretend, person who has superhuman powers and uses them to do bad things.

22

For More Information

Books

Bray, Adam. *Marvel Studios 101: All Your Questions Answered*. New York, NY: DK Publishing, 2018.

Hutchison, Patricia. *The Science of Superheroes*. Minneapolis, MN: Core Library, 2017.

Websites

Chris Hemsworth
www.biography.com/actor/chris-hemsworth
Read more about Chris on this website.

Thor
www.marvel.com/characters/thor-thor-odinson/on-screen
Learn all about Chris's character Thor here.

★ *Index* ★

actor, 4, 5, 6, 17
Australia, 4, 6, 7, 8, 16, 18, 20
Australian Childhood Foundation, 18, 19
Avengers, 4, 11, 13
brothers, 4, 5, 6, 7, 9
bushfires, 19
charities, 18
daughter, 16
father, 4
Ghostbusters, 15
high school, 6
Home and Away, 7
Men in Black: International, 14
money, 6, 13, 18
mother, 4
Pataky, Elsa, 16, 17
Rush, 15
Snow White and the Huntsman, 15
sports, 16
Thompson, Tessa, 15
Thor: Love and Thunder, 20
Thor: Ragnarok, 12, 15
Thor, 4, 8, 9, 10, 11, 12, 13, 14, 15, 20
Tourism Australia, 16
twins, 16
United States, 7, 8
Vacation, 15